Gemma

Alice

birthday cake

yum!

The Official
Jacqueline Wilson
Mag

D0590779

What's Inside...

EMAIL: jwmag@dcthomson.co.uk

POST: JW Mag, PO Box 305, London, NW1 1TX

WEB: www.jw-mag.com

Text and illustrations © 2010 Jacqueline Wilson and Nick Sharratt. Printed and published by D.C.Thomson & Co., Ltd.,185 Fleet Street, London EC4A 2HS. ©D.C.Thomson, 2010. Whilst every reasonable care will be taken neither D.C Thomson & Co., Ltd., nor its agents accept liability for loss or damage to material submitted to this publication. No part of this magazine may be reproduced without prior written permission.

This super-cool totally terrific annual belongs to

MY FAVOURITES!

food _Gammon shank_

pet _Guinea pig/cat_

colour _Blue_

hobby _Drawing/Red_

jw book _Lily Alone_

Hi everyone! ♡

Welcome to the very first <u>Official Jacqueline Wilson Mag Annual</u>. I'm so excited! I've always loved annuals. I've kept some special ones ever since I was a child, and still love flicking through the well—thumbed pages. I wonder if any of you will keep this annual until you have children of your own?

You'll see a picture of my lovely daughter Emma in the special picture gallery. Do you think we look alike? I used to make up all sorts of stories for Emma when she was little and then she'd write me little illustrated booklets in return. It's great that so many of you like writing and drawing. You'll find all sorts of fun tips in this annual to create your own characters. You'll also see how to design your very own magazine! It would be wonderful if some of you send us your finished copy. We might even feature it some time!

I've written a special new story for the annual. It was fun writing a slightly different time—shift story. I wonder which of my stories you like best? Please do write in and tell me. I love to receive your letters and your fantastic drawings. You can learn how to draw five of my all—time favourite characters in this annual — <u>Pearl, Alice, Beauty and the twins, Ruby and Garnet.</u>

How many characters do you think I've actually invented? I've written nearly a hundred books, so that must mean thousands of characters! It's weird thinking of all those people springing out of my imagination. But whenever people say my name there's often just one character people think of and that's dear old Tracy Beaker! If Tracy were real she'd be leaping up and down joyously because she's the main girl on the cover of this annual!

I've always felt particularly fond of Tracy because it was her book that became a best seller and a hugely popular TV series. There's a great feature in the annual which shows you how to make a pretty ribbon friendship bracelet. Maybe I should make a very special bracelet for my oldest and dearest character friend, Tracy Beaker.

Happy reading, everyone!

Love from

Jacqueline Wilson

Jacky's Photo

Early Years

Jacky with her mum and dad in 1946.

Playing outside with her beloved dolls.

Aww! It's Jacky's baby picture. So sweet!

"This was taken for a newspaper article. My mum was very proud that we were going to be in the paper."

"I've always adored dolls."

With best friend, Chris, aged 15.

This is Jacky with the actress Mandy Miller.

"I love an old black and white movie called Mandy and this girl played her. I was so excited to meet her!"

"We're still friends now."

Album

It's her life in pictures!

JW

Jacky was always writing!

At school with her favourite teacher, Mr Townsend.

"I spent all my pocket money on notebooks and pencils."

Jacky in the office at her first job. She became a magazine journalist after leaving secretarial school.

Jacky's wedding day! Getting marred to Millar when she was 19.

Jacky with her own beautiful daughter, Emma.

"This is my favourite photo of the two of us."

9

JW

It's JW with JK Rowling!

Jacky's very first award...

The Suitcase Kid

Jacqueline Wilson

"We were at the Queen's 80th birthday celebrations in Buckingham Palace Gardens."

"I won the Children's Book Award for The Suitcase Kid in 1992."

A more recent pic of Jacky and her daughter, Emma.

"This is me with my illustrator, Nick Sharratt. I'm very pleased and proud that we work together!"

With Michelle Collins and Alice Connor who played Marigold and Dolphin in *The Illustrated Mum.*

At the fair!

"I'm very fond of hobby horses!"

Jacky at work!

"This is the study of my old house, where I wrote so many books!"

"Here I am in my last house. There's hardly enough room for all my books..."

Jacky on a recent trip to Dubai.

"I had a wonderful time!"

Jacky wins lots of prizes! This is a DBE, the prize she received when she was made a Dame.

JW

11

Fact File Pearl

Hi, I'm Pearl!

"This is me and my big sister Jodie at my eleventh birthday party."

"My friend Harley and I love watching badgers."

"One of my birthday presents was a journal. I like to write all my stories and secrets in it."

"This is Melchester College, the school where I met my friend Harley."

13

How To Draw Pearl

Learn how to draw a seated character in just six steps.

1

Outline an egg shape for Pearl's head and sketch the shape of her body. Draw an open book in her lap.

2

Draw in the lines of the bath to make Pearl look as though she is sitting down. Add the details of her dressing gown.

Use a wavy line to draw in the bubbles and Pearl's fluffy dressing gown. Give her long sweeping hair and add her hands.

3

Colour her in using yellow for her hair and pink for her dressing gown.

4

Add detail to Pearl's dressing gown and her hair. Sketch in her pen and the writing in her book.

5

Draw in Pearl's facial features and shade in the cover of the book. Use horizontal and vertical lines to create the tiles in the background.

6

Tip: Shade in areas by drawing lots of lines in one direction then drawing over it with lines in the opposite direction.

Written by **Jacqueline Wilson**

THE VICTORIAN BRIDESMAID'S DRESS

Lisa has to wear a very weird bridesmaid's dress, but that's not all that's strange about Aunt Vicky's wedding...

I'm very disappointed in the bridesmaid's dress when I first see it. I've been longing and longing to be a bridesmaid for ages. My best friend, Laura, was a bridesmaid last year and she wore a pink satin dress with matching satin shoes and a little ring of rosebuds in her hair. My second best friend, Anna, was a bridesmaid last winter, and she wore a red velvet dress with a little furry cape and a gold necklace with a *real* ruby in it!

I ache to wear pink satin or red velvet — but my bridesmaid's dress is a weird pale grey silk, with bunchy, buttoned sleeves, a long skirt and a waist so tight I can hardly breathe.

"Mum! Has Aunt Vicky gone nuts? Who wants to wear *grey*? It's the colour of school uniforms!" I say, trying to undo all the tiny little buttons again.

"Hey, careful, Lisa, you'll pull those buttons off! Let me have a proper look at you. Oh yes, you look a picture.

16

Illustrated by Nick Sharratt

"Goodness knows how your cousin Lucy is going to cope though — you know the way she's always stuffing chocolates and crisps. She's going to have to wear a corset to get into *her* dress," says Mum. (Neither of us can stick my cousin Lucy!)

"Why does Aunt Vicky want us to wear such peculiar old-fashioned bridesmaid dresses?"

"That's the point! I told you, she's having her wedding at Greenfield Castle. It's Victorian — Queen Victoria actually stayed there once for a weekend. It's furnished Victorian style, ever so grand. So our Vicky wants her wedding there, and she's wearing a specially made Victorian dress, with six bridesmaids and a little flower girl in fancy clothes too. It's costing a fortune but it'll look gorgeous in the photos."

Mum sighs. She had a small wedding with a reception in a pub and the photos were taken by Dad's best mate and came out all blurry.

I'm still not sure about my bridesmaid's dress on Aunt Vicky's wedding day. I feel a right banana getting into our car on Saturday morning with half the kids on our estate giggling because I look so odd in my prim pale grey. But when we get to Greenfield Castle I actually see Aunt Vicky's point.

The castle is an amazing Victorian building with turrets and towers. Inside it's tremendously grand, with crimson wallpaper and chandeliers and velvet sofas and chairs. There are lots of portraits of top-hatted men with moustaches and ladies with piled up hair and simpering smiles.

There are heaps of photographs too — long rectangles of Victorian schoolchildren sitting cross-legged, Victorian cricket teams, Victorian young men and ladies punting on the river, and even a real Victorian wedding with a bride and a groom and bridesmaids.

Greenfield Castle

I glance at the wedding photo, and just for a moment this strange shiver goes through me. I feel really sick and dizzy and stand still, my head spinning.

"Lisa? Are you all right?" Mum asks.

"Well, I feel a bit sick."

"You're not allowed to be sick, not wearing that dress! Here, have a peppermint. It's probably just the excitement."

17

I start feeling fine again as we go up the long stairs to the room where Aunty Vicky and all the other bridesmaids are getting ready. Aunt Vicky looks so *different*. She usually has a short haircut, and she wears very short skirts too, but now she's got hair extensions piled up on her head, with a filmy white train hanging down. Her dress is so long it trails on the ground in pale snowy drifts.

"You look just like a real Victorian bride, Aunt Vicky!" I say.

"And you look the very picture of a Victorian bridesmaid," Aunt Vicky replies. She looks round quickly at all my cousins. "You all look wonderful, girls," she says.

Cousin Lucy certainly looks less than wonderful crammed into her dress, her face bright red with effort,

but the others look okay. We all have our hair brushed and swept up into a topknot affair by the hair-stylist.

Oh dear, now it's Lucy's turn to look down her nose at me. Her long straight hair goes into a perfect topknot, with the back part trailing demurely round her shoulders. My mad frizz won't do as it's told, even though the stylist brushes till my scalp tingles. It explodes out of its topknot and sticks out wildly. I get a bit fussed about it, but Aunt Vicky gives me a hug and says I look gorgeous even so.

"You'd better stand at the end of the line when we have our photos taken. Then they can cut you from the picture if they think your hair looks too silly," says Lucy.

"Cheek! *You're* the one who'll spoil the photo. It'll be the bride, five

Great Auntie Margaret

bridesmaids, one flower girl, and one grey hippo," I say.

Lucy shoves me and I shove back and several buttons pop on my sleeve.

"Girls, girls, girls!" says Great Auntie Margaret, Aunt Vicky's Mum. She's wearing a weird purple costume and a daft hat like a giant frisbee. Maybe it isn't a good idea to have a Victorian wedding!

But when order is restored and Aunt Vicky walks slowly down the great staircase, all us bridesmaids following, everyone gasps and goes "Aaaah!" Aunt Vicky's fiancé Mike is all got up in a tail coat with gold brocade waistcoat and looks very dashing. They get married in the big hall, with all of us watching, sitting on little gilt chairs. The service is very romantic and lovely and nearly all the ladies cry. Great Auntie Margaret sobs so much her hat falls off!

Then we go out through the French windows on to the veranda to have our wedding photos taken. Great Auntie Margaret starts bossing us all about to stand in the correct order. She tuts again at my hair, and then sees some of my sleeve buttons have popped off.

"Oh, for pity's sake, Lisa! Where did those buttons go? Run back up to the dressing room and have a good look on the floor. I've got a needle and a thread in my handbag," she says.

"They won't show, Auntie Margaret. I can always put my hands behind my back," I say.

"Don't be so silly. Go on, move! We don't want to keep the photographer waiting."

I sigh, and rush off. I go back indoors. It's weirdly quiet because everyone's outside and I seem to have lost my bearings. I don't know what's happened to all the little gilt chairs in the wedding room. The hall looks different too.

Perhaps there are two halls, because this one's dark green, and there are sad and creepy stag's heads everywhere, peering down at me with their glass eyes. I know the dressing room's on the first floor, so I dash up the stairs but the carpet's different too — brighter and madly patterned.

Now I can't find the right dressing room. These are all bedrooms, with those big four-poster beds. There's a strange bathroom too, with a vast mahogany-seat toilet. I'm rather in need of it, so I quickly use it. I can't work out how to flush it. But then I pull a little plug and water swooshes over the willow pattern inside.

I peer at it, fascinated.

"Lisa, Lisa! Are you in there, child? Do hurry up, the photographer is waiting!"

I hurry out — and stare at the complete stranger. She's got a funny hat like Great Auntie Margaret's, and a dark striped dress. Is she some other Great Auntie, come especially for the wedding?

She seems to know me anyway. She takes hold of me and hurries me downstairs.

Not Aunt Vicky!

"I'm supposed to be looking for my buttons," I say, showing her my flapping sleeve.

She makes little tutting noises with her teeth.

"You are a trial to us all, Lisa! Well, there's no time to search for them now. The photographer is becoming most impatient."

She whisks me right down the bright carpet, through the green hall under the stag's heads, and then out onto the veranda. The whole wedding party is assembled. But what's going on? Why have they changed their clothes? They're all wearing Victorian outfits now, not just Aunt Vicky and Mike and my cousins.

Hang on, who are all those girls in grey bridesmaid's dresses? Where's cousin Lucy? And that bride in her long white frock — she's not Aunt Vicky! It's someone else entirely, a pinched-face pale lady who's frowning at me.

"Really, Lisa, do come along! Oh my goodness, your hair! And your sleeves! I wish I hadn't chosen you as a bridesmaid now."

"But I — I'm not your bridesmaid!" I stammer.

They're all frowning at me now.

"Don't be ridiculous, girl! Stand up straight, next to your cousins," the older lady commands me.

I'm pushed and prodded into line, and then we're all told to look at the photographer. He's in Victorian costume too — and he's using a huge Victorian camera. He has to duck underneath a black velvet curtain to take our photo, while we're told to stay very, very still. We're not even supposed to blink. I do my best — but my topknot hair is starting to tumble down. I put my hand up to adjust it, just as the camera flashes. Whoops!

The older lady with the mad hat has seen me moving.

"You're going out of your way to spoil this wedding! Wait till we get you home, Lisa! You will be severely whipped."

Whipped? Something tells me she's not joking! And this isn't a mock Victorian wedding. This is real! I've suddenly stepped back a hundred and fifty years into the past! But I know one thing. I'm not staying here!

I start running as fast as I can in my stupid tight dress.

"Hey! Come back at once, Lisa! How dare you run off!"

I take no notice and make for the French windows. I hurtle through them — and oh joy, oh wonder, it's the room with all the gilt chairs, and there's cousin Lucy glaring at me.

"Where have you been, Lisa? I've been sent to find you."

"Oh Lucy!" I say, and I hug her hard.

"Are you mad?" she says, because we've been deadly enemies ever since we were little. "Come on, everyone's waiting for you!"

She pulls me back towards the French window.

"No! I'm not going out there again!" I say — but then I see Mum and Dad through the glass, I see Aunt Vicky and Mike and all the other bridesmaids, and a trendy photographer in his black t—shirt and jeans, clicking away like crazy.

"Come on, or we won't be in the photos!" says Lucy.

I hang onto her hand and go out onto the veranda. Everything's perfectly safe and ordinary and I'm at my real Aunt's wedding and it's 2010. I stand in line and smile and end up in almost every photo in Aunt Vicky's white wedding album.

But I'm in another photo too. When we go back inside for reception, we pause in the red—papered hall, looking at the portraits and photographs. I stare again at the Victorian wedding photo.

There's a bride and a groom, a fierce looking woman in a silly hat, a little row of bridesmaids — and right at the end there's one more bridesmaid in a long grey dress. Her face is a blur because she's moved when the photo was taken. But it's easy to make out her lifted arm with a flapping sleeve and her untidy frizzy hair tumbling out of the topknot.

The End

21

Use Jacky's special guide to put your own story together. Who knows — you could be the next big author!

J.W.'s Story

What's your story about?

Jacky says... I wonder what sort of story you like writing best? I like to write realistic stories — sometimes they're funny, sometimes they're sad. You might like to write a fantasy — or perhaps a scary story? You decide.

Your big opening line

Jacky says... It's very important to have an attention—grabbing opening line. The main thing is to make people want to read more. Try to write one here.

The beginning

Jacky says... Sometimes a blank sheet of paper can be rather scary. The best thing to do is to get started, then you can always come back and change things later. I know I do! Write your first paragraph.

Maker!

You've read my short story, now it's your turn!

The middle

Special Tip!

Decide if you're writing in the 'first person' (so you say 'I' and write from the point of view of your main character) or in the 'third person' (so you talk about your character and use their name).

Jacky says... This is where you develop your story and the main action happens. Think back to what your story is about and decide what the details will be. Just let your imagination go and keep writing. Use extra paper if you need it.

23

JW's Story

The end

Jacky says... Now you need to tie everything together and bring the story to an end. Do you want a happy ending where everything works out? Or do you want a shock ending that takes the reader by surprise? See which works best for your story.

What does your main character look like?

Jacky says... I wish I could draw like Nick Sharratt! I *do* always have a clear idea of my characters and know what they look like. Picture your main character and try to draw them here.

24

Maker!

Your amazing title

Jacky says... Now you need to decide what to call your story. I usually name my books after the main character or theme of the book. You could try that, or you could pick anything you want. It can even be a silly title, but as long as it tells your readers something about your story, that's fine.

Your storybook cover!

Jacky says... Have a bit of fun and imagine what the cover of your story would be if it was made into a book. I love the way Nick designs my covers, so you can try something like that or come up with something just for you.

Special Tip!

Nick did a fantastic job with *Little Darlings* by making it look like a showbiz magazine. Can you think of a clever design for your own cover?

PUZZLE?

Can you find Jacqueline Wilson's characters hidden in the grid?

Cookie
Justine
Biscuits
Ruby
Tracy Beaker
Jodie
Vicky Angel
Sunset
Garnet
Pearl
Cam
Verity
Hetty Feather
Destiny

```
L E C L Y G Y Z S G A H C N O
Z E R O A S E O T L E J V H D
E R G R O N D E S T I N Y L B
I I N N I K E P T J H B R R D
X E D T A S I Y Q Q U M T A I
T O S O Z Y F E T R S C G E K
M U F C J E K C A M T N I P E
J Z V T A B W C M D I S K T P
T W S T A B S I I Y U U D C K
D P H X T E M N J V C N B O E
X E C W K E V K Q B S S O G G
R U S U T F X E F L I E T D Y
U M Z M W G Y X Z E B T P A V
R E K A E B Y C A R T H P I I
Y T I R E V X U V T F M G D B
```

26

TIME!

Use Tracy's code to learn more about your favourite characters

Now you can write your own secret messages to your friends!

27

Talent?

WINTER

LOVE

SPIDERS

FAME

POPCORN

STRAWBERRY

CHOCOLATE

You daydream about...

Your bedroom is...

Your favourite shoes are...

NEAT & TIDY

A MESS

TRAINERS

PUMPS

WRITING

You've got a natural flair for creating vivid characters and imaginative stories. Take a leaf out of **Hetty**'s book and start scribbling your thoughts, ideas and stories in a special notebook.

SINGING

Wow! You love to make people smile and dream of singing in front of hundreds and thousands of adoring fans. Your talent for singing could even give Destiny a run for her money!

ACTING

Watch out Hollywood! Like **Tracy**, you love to be the centre of attention and performing on stage is your ultimate dream. Better start practising your glam red carpet poses in the mirror now!

DANCING

Just like Jodie, you love to move around and show off your cool dance moves to anyone who'll watch! Why not get a few friends together and start your very own dance group?

CREDIT IMAGE - Thinkstock

The biggest and best JACQUELINE WILSON INTERVIEW ever!

1 What's your best advice for someone who wants to be a writer?

I suggest you read lots — not to copy ideas, but to enrich your imagination and increase your vocabulary. I've never met a writer who isn't a total bookworm.

2 What is the happiest moment from your writing career?

I think it was when a girl from a children's home told me that my books had made her love reading, and my character Tracy Beaker had raised her status with the other kids at school. They thought it was now pretty cool to be in care.

3 Have you ever had a book turned down?

Yes, twice — and I was devastated both times! But it's something you just have to accept — and start all over again on a new book. Luckily this hasn't happened for a long time!

4 Are any of your characters based on yourself?

No — apart from Jenna Williams!

5 Do you dislike any of your characters?

I invent some really mean characters, like Kim in Bad Girls and Rhiannon in Candyfloss — but there's always a reason why they're so horrid so I don't actually dislike them.

6 Who is your best friend?

My best friend is Trish. We both love reading and the cinema and going for long walks in the park.

7 What do you think it takes to be a best friend?

You have to be supportive to each other — and it's always great if you laugh at the same things.

8 If you hadn't become an author, what would you be?

I'd love to have been an illustrator, but I'm not talented enough. I'd also like to have my own bookshop!

9 What gave you the inspiration for Hetty Feather?

The Foundling Museum asked if I could possibly write a special book for them. I wasn't sure I would have the time to do all the research — but then I became seriously ill and I had to convalesce for months, so I had a wonderful time lolling on the sofa reading many Victorian books. The character of Hetty Feather bounced fully—formed into my brain, and I knew I had to write her story.

Jacqueline Wilson
LOLA ROSE
Illustrated by Nick Sharratt

10 Which book has been the hardest to write?

I think it was Lola Rose — it's such a sad book, though it does have a happy ending. I always try to be honest when I write about troubling subjects, but I don't want my books to be too upsetting.

12 What's your favourite thing about having your own magazine?

It's a wonderful way to stay in touch with my readers (and I get to try out all the yummy recipes!).

11 ...and what about Little Darlings?

I've often wondered what it would be like to be the child of a very famous celebrity, so I invented Sunset, who absolutely hates all the attention she attracts.

31

And now...

the silly questions you would be too scared to ask!

1

What's your favourite fairground ride?

I adore old-fashioned carousels.

2 How long have you worn glasses?

Since I was ten. The first day I wore them my teacher called me 'four-eyes' — a nickname I hated. I used to dislike wearing glasses, but now they're so much a part of me I couldn't bear to be without them.

3 Why do you always wear black?

I've worn black (with lots of silver jewellery) because I've always thought it a cool look — but over the last couple of years I've branched out a little! I've got blue outfits, even green... maybe I'll be wearing all the colours of the rainbow when I'm an old lady.

4 What's the most scared you have ever been?

When my beloved daughter Emma was seriously ill. Thank goodness she got completely better.

5 Do you make lots of money as an author?

I made very little money for twenty years or more — but then I got very lucky and now I do make lots of money, though I do have to work very hard.

32

6 If you were the Queen for a day, what would you do?

I'd invite hundreds of children to the Palace and throw a huge party. I'd let very special children try on my crown.

7 What's the best thing you have ever bought?

I think it has to be my house. I first saw it when I was three years old. My Grandma and I used to walk down the street looking at all these lovely houses, trying to decide which one we'd choose if we ever got really rich. We decided which house we liked the most — and now, many years later, I've been able to buy it.

8 Is there a book by somebody else that you wish you had written?

I'd have loved to have written many of Katherine Mansfield's short stories. I also wished I'd written Where the Wild Things Are even though it's only 338 words long (but with brilliant illustrations).

9 You're so good at writing... is there anything you're really bad at?

I'm useless at Maths and filling in forms and I can barely use a computer.

10 If you had a super power, what would it be?

I'd love to be able to fly.

11 If you had to eat the same food for the rest of your life, what would it be?

Easy — buttery mashed potatoes!

12 If you could only take three things on holiday, what would you take?

Books, my swimsuit and some spending money!

How To Draw Alice

Learn how to draw a full-length character in just four easy steps.

1 Start with an oval shape for Alice's head. Outline her top and skirt and draw in her hair so that it ends just above her sleeves.

Tip: Make Alice's legs the same length as her top.

2 Add Alice's arms and hands. Outline the shape of her legs.

3 Draw in Alice's facial features. Then add a flower design to her top and skirt and give her strappy shoes.

4 Now colour her in. Alice has rosy cheeks and blonde hair.

36

Now it's your turn!

Design Your Cover!

It's very important to get the right look for your cover because it sets the mood for your whole magazine. Look at my cover for the first ever issue of my magazine. It's very bright and has lots going on. The main things you'll need for your cover are...

A fabulous ☆ logo ☆
Make it bright and colourful

A tagline
What's special about your mag? Say it in one line!

Special gifts ☆
Will you have any free gifts with your mag?

A cover star ★
What about using your favourite character?

☆ Fun ☆ features
What would you like to see inside?

IT'S MY NEW MAG!

FREE ☑BOOK – Sneak peek at Jacky's NEW
☑NOTEBOOK ☑PEN

Jacqueline Wilson
LITTLE DARLINGS

The Official Jacqueline Wilson Mag

ISSUE No.1

STORY BY JACQUELINE WILSON

WIN! MEET JACKY! INSIDE

BOOK OF THE MONTH
CRAFTS
QUIZZES
REAL LIFE PROBLEMS

TRACY BEAKER RETURNS!

FOR GIRLS WHO ♥ READING!

40 You may also want to include some cute pictures, special interviews, and some craft ideas – whatever you want!

Now it's your turn! Work on the design for your perfect magazine here . . .

Totally EMBARRASSING!

Help finish this page of cringes. Fill in the boxes with you and your friends' embarrassing moments and add a rating!

Red Face Ratings!

☆☆☆ So shaming! ★★★★ No way!
★★★★★ Major blush!

Blushing Bloomers!

My friends dared me to run to the bottom of the garden with a pair of my mum's big frilly pants on my head at a sleepover one night. I was halfway to the bottom of the garden when all of a sudden the security light came on. I almost died of embarrassment when I spotted my next door neighbour laughing hysterically from his bedroom window. Now he calls me Little Miss Granny Pants!

Siobhan, Hereford

Red face rating: ☆☆☆

Title here

Red face rating:

42

Crying Shame!

I was with my class on the way home from a school trip when I fell fast asleep on the bus. Suddenly, I was woken by someone crying and shouting for their mummy. I was looking around to see who it was when I realised that everyone on the bus was laughing at me and calling me a big baby - I must've had a bad dream and cried out for my mum in my sleep! Cringe!

Bernie, Manchester

Add an illustration here!

Red face rating: ★ ★ ★ ★

Hot Dog Horror!

I was watching a really funny film at the cinema with my friends and laughing so hard I accidentally jolted my friend's arm and sent her hot dog flying through the air. We thought it had fallen onto the floor until the lights came on at the end of the film and we spotted it in the hood of a man's jacket! He hadn't noticed and I just couldn't face telling him!

Julia, Cornwall

Red face rating: ★ ★ ★ ★ ★

Red face rating:

Changing Room Cringe!

I was with my BF in our favourite clothing store and we were trying on silly outfits and parading round the changing room. I was so busy showing off I bumped right into a mannequin. Her head fell to the floor and her nose broke clean off! I was so embarrassed I haven't been back to the store since!

Sonia, Rotherham

Red face rating: ★ ★ ★ ★

Red face rating:

43

Make Your Own

FLOWCHART!

Vicky   Jodie   Gemma

Have you always wanted to make your very own fun quizzes to try out on your friends? Use this flowchart for inspiration and follow our simple guide!

Who's Your Fashion Match?

START

Your diary is filled with doodles of...

FLOWERS →

SOOOO BORING →

Which endangered animal do you love?

Glossy fashion magazines are...

SKULL & CROSSBONES

TIGER

DOLPHIN

INSPIRATIONAL

The clothes hanging in your wardrobe are...

The suitcase you're packing is nearly full. What do you squeeze in?

TRUTH

Truth or Dare?

ORGANISED

CLUTTERED

DARE

JEANS

HIGH HEELS

A FASHIONISTA VICKY
You have a natural flair for fashion and love to co-ordinate your outfits with fabulous accessories. Like Vicky, you could spend hours in the shops, trying on hundreds of gorgeous outfits!

B UNIQUE JODIE
You're not afraid to experiment with fashion and you love to shock people with your latest look! You're great at adding unusual accessories to get your outfit just right.

C CASUAL GEMMA
Comfortable and clean is your fashion style — who has time for glamour?! You're far too busy having fun with your BF in your comfy old jeans to bother with sparkly tops and bling hair clips.

44

Now it's your turn!

Which animal are you?

Give your chart a title — it should be a question.

Draw a fun illustration!

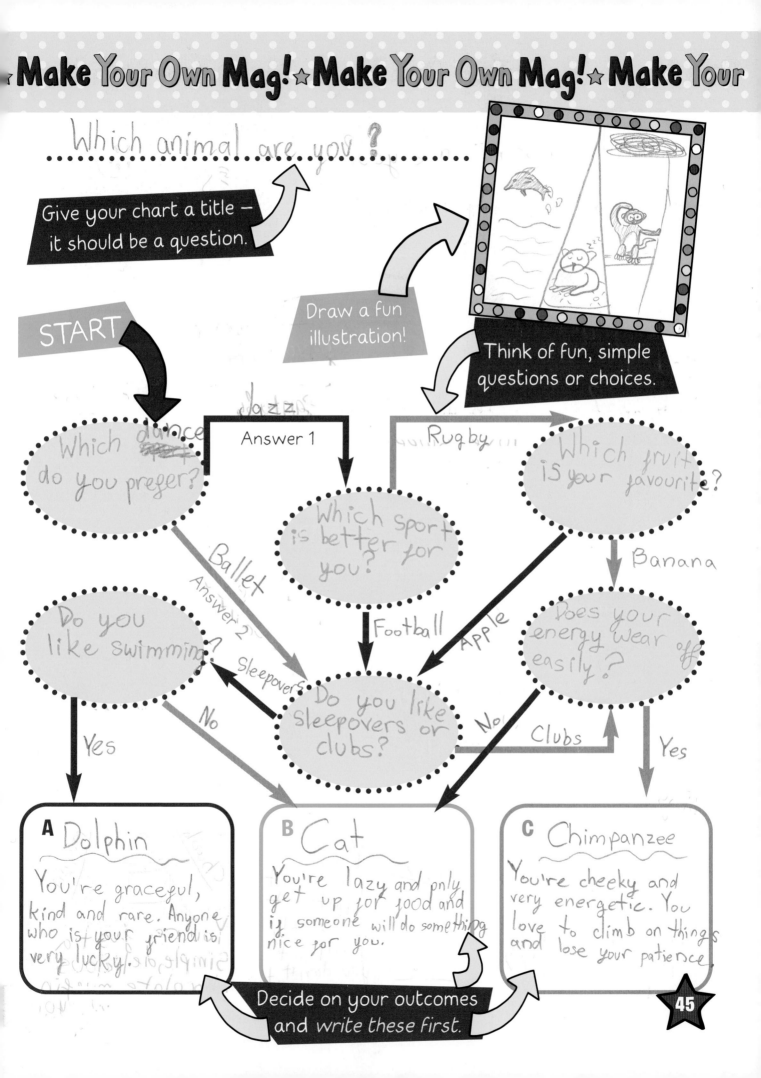

Think of fun, simple questions or choices.

START

Which dance do you prefer?

Jazz

Answer 1

Rugby

Which fruit is your favourite?

Which sport is better for you?

Ballet

Answer 2

Banana

Do you like swimming?

Sleepovers

Football

Apple

Does your energy wear off easily?

Do you like sleepovers or clubs?

No

No

Clubs

Yes

Yes

A Dolphin

You're graceful, kind and rare. Anyone who is your friend is very lucky.

B Cat

You're lazy and only get up for food and if someone will do something nice for you.

C Chimpanzee

You're cheeky and very energetic. You love to climb on things and lose your patience.

Decide on your outcomes and *write these first.*

45

...Which dessert are you?...

START

Stuck for question ideas? Think of **choices** like 'Is Cookie better than Little Darlings?'

You could stick a photo here.

Are you kind to others?

Y

Do you love sweet things?

Is your favourite book type fantasy?

N

Do you love rainbows and unicorns?

N

Y

Do you kiss anyone goodnight?

Y

Do you regularly go to the kitchen for food?

Y

Draw pictures in these boxes.

Do you spend time with your family?

Y

N

Do you like simple stuff?

N

Y

N

Y

Sour gummy sweet.

Your personality is cruel and you need to change or you'll have no friends!

Lemon meringue

Your personality might not be exactly great but if you ~~try~~ more, you'll be perfect!

Chocolate muffin

Try it out yourself to make sure your outcome makes sense!

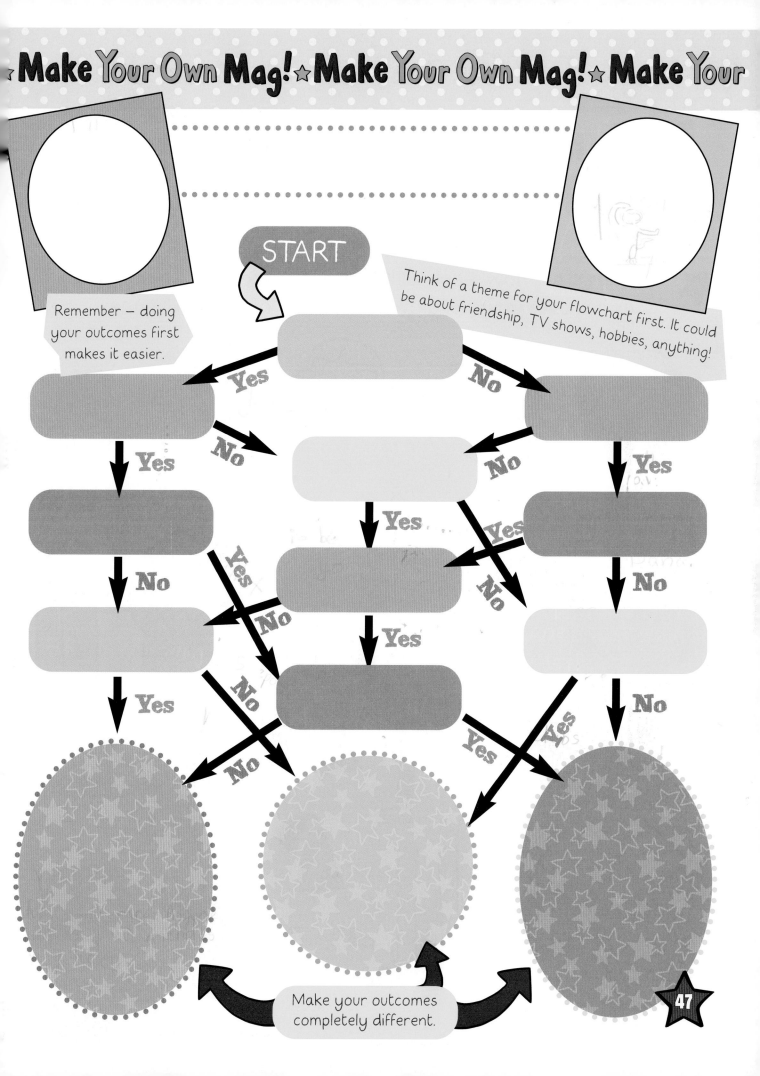

START

Remember – doing your outcomes first makes it easier.

Think of a theme for your flowchart first. It could be about friendship, TV shows, hobbies, anything!

Yes

No

Yes

No

Yes

No

Yes

Yes

No

Yes

No

No

Yes

Yes

No

No

Yes

Yes

No

Make your outcomes completely different.

47

Design Your Own CHARACTER

Would you just love to do mag illustrations like Nick Sharratt? You can start now! Look at the bits 'n' pieces below for ideas and create your very own character on the next page.

My Masterpiece!

MY BOOK REVIEW!

A good book review will be an interesting part of your new mag. Try it here!

Title ....

Draw your book cover here!

Who is in the book? Describe them

The main characters are ....
....
....
....

50

My favourite character is ....
because ....
....

Why is this character your favourite? Is it their personality? Do you admire how they coped in a difficult situation? Does the character make you feel happy or sad?

Storyline ....
....
....
....

What happened in the book? Think about the main events.

The best bit ....
....
....

Think about which part of the book moved you most. It might have been a really sad or emotional part, or even something that made you laugh out loud!

Is there anything about the story that you'd love to change? How about the ending or one of the characters?

What would you change? ....
....
....
....

RATE IT! Colour in the stars to rate your book out of five.

Which JW Character Is Your Style Sister?

Try our fun tick quiz to find out!

Tick your favourite pictures to create an outfit you'd love to wear. Then add up the colours so you can find out who your character style match is!

Mostly Blue

You are confident and bold, just like Elsa, who loves her stylish cowgirl look. You know that the most important things in life are friends and family so people know you're super-sweet. You don't mind being different, which is why you can sometimes surprise people.

Mostly Red

It's a cool and casual look for you, so you match with Tracy's tomboy style. You're not really into spending hours in front of the mirror... there are so many more fun things to do! Your chilled out personality is the reason why all your friends love hanging out with you.

Mostly Pink

Jodie is fashion crazy and loves being totally on trend, just like you! You love being the centre of attention and it shows in your bubbly personality. If there is a party happening, you will always be the first one invited... which is great because you LOVE parties!

Mostly Green

Your edgy Rock Chick style makes you stand out in the crowd, just like Destiny from *Little Darlings*. There is never a dull moment when you're around and all your friends just love your daring style. You're a little star in the making, so keep challenging yourself to try new things!

Can you fit the yummy grub into the Sudoku grid? Each row, column and mini-grid must only contain one picture of each tasty treat.

Answer:

Yum yum, slurp slurp!

How To Draw Cookie

Learn how to draw Cookie's portrait in just four easy steps.

1 In faint pencil draw a squared oval for Cookie's head. Add her shoulders and the outline of her collar and tie.

2 Draw in Cookie's hair and give her a side parting. Add three small ovals for her hair clip.

3 Fill in Cookie's facial features and give her a stripy tie. Add lines to her hair and four short lines on her forehead for a fringe.

4 Finish by colouring her in. Cookie's school tie is brown with red and yellow stripes.

Tip: You can change the look on Cookie's face by drawing her eyebrows in a different position and changing her mouth.

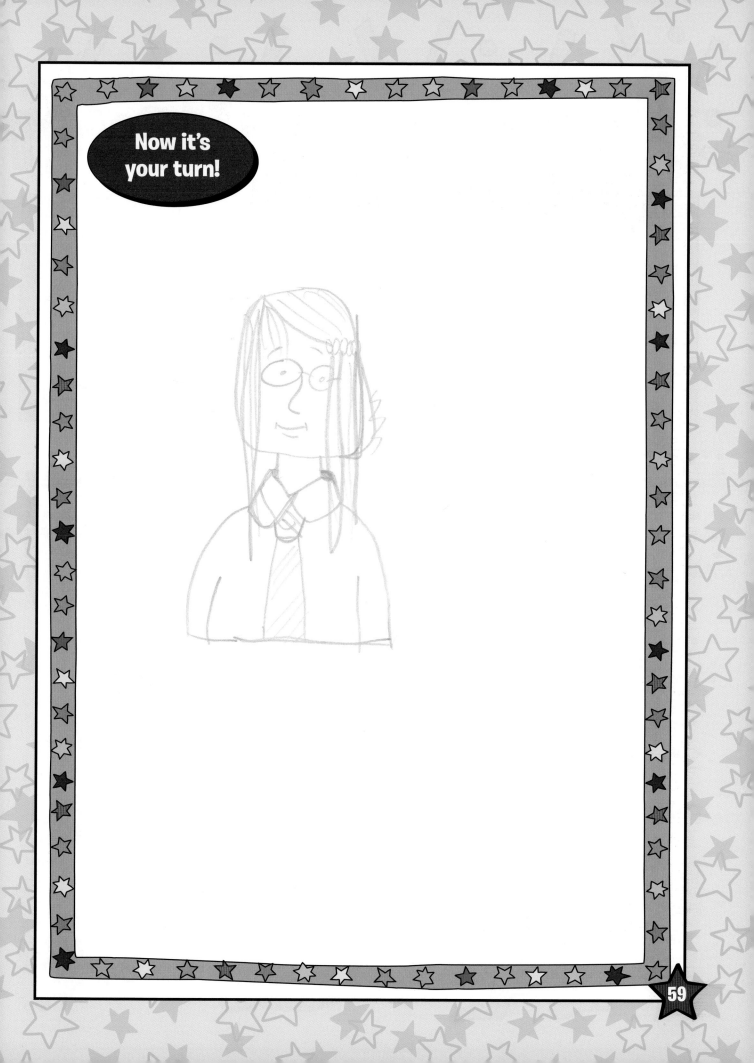

Now it's
your turn!

Are You A Clever

How To Play

❶ Spend 20 seconds looking at all the pictures on these pages (use your mobile phone or watch to time it!). ❷ Now close the book and write down as many of the Cookie items you can remember... no peeking! ❸ Add up your score to see if you have a mega memory! Which ones did you forget? ❹ Now ask your family and friends to try - we bet you'll beat them all!

squeak!

milkshake

yum!

monster from Mars!

60

Cookie?

Play just like Cookie! See how many of these cool pictures you can remember with our fun memory game.

£1000

birthday cake *yum!*

sweeties

yum!

burger

jelly *spider*

yum!

yum!

61

The biggest and best NICK SHARRATT INTERVIEW ever!

Nick's set design!

1 What's your best advice for someone who wants to be an illustrator?

Well, for a start you've absolutely got to love to draw! Just about all of my illustrator friends knew they were going to be artists from a very early age because they adored drawing so much.

2 Did you always know that this would be your job?

I wanted to be an artist way back at primary school. In fact I can pinpoint the exact day I made up my mind about my future career. One of my pictures had been pinned up in the school hall — the husband of one of my teachers saw it and commissioned me to draw a similar picture for him. He paid me £5. I thought 'what a wonderful way to earn a living!'

3 If you hadn't become an artist, what would you be?

The only other jobs I've ever done were paperboy and working in a brewery cellar when I was a student so I think I'd have to choose between them! Actually I did like making model stage sets when I was a teenager, so perhaps I could have become a set designer.

4 How did you start working with Jacqueline Wilson?

We had both worked separately with the same editor who then had the idea of putting us together for The Story of Tracy Beaker. We went out for lunch and Jacqueline says she was satisfied that I'd be the right person to illustrate Tracy when she saw the dazzling yellow socks I was wearing!

5 Is she one of your best friends?

Jacqueline is a very dear friend. We've been on holidays together and shared some great times.

Jacky

Nick

Photo by Trish Beswick

6 How do you decide what a character will look like?

With Jacqueline's books I read the manuscript three or four times, and by the time I've finished I've usually found enough clues in the text to work out how the characters should look.

7 Which character do you love drawing most?

Tracy Beaker is my favourite. But I really enjoyed illustrating Hetty Feather too, and taking on the challenge of conveying her personality with silhouettes.

8 Which character is the trickiest to get right?

I find teenage boys quite tricky to draw. It takes a lot of attempts to get them right. Thinking about it, Harley in My Sister Jodie was pretty difficult.

9 You've written some of your own children's books too. Which is your favourite?

It could be Moo–Cow, Kung–Fu–Cow, it could be Ketchup on your Cornflakes?, it could be Don't Put Your Finger In The Jelly, Nelly!. As you can see, I like silly titles and my favourite subjects are animals and food.

10 How did you come up with your drawing style?

It's simply my natural way of drawing. If you were to look at the pictures I drew as a schoolboy you'd see that they're not all that different to my work now. I've always liked drawing in quite a graphic way, using a black line and bright, flat colours.

11 What are the best and worst things about your job?

Being my own boss, stretching my imagination daily, and the thrill of spotting a young reader engrossed in a book I've illustrated are all fantastic things about my job. The worst thing is being under huge pressure sometimes to meet all my deadlines.

Nick painting, age 6.

12 What's your favourite thing about The Official Jacqueline Wilson Mag?

Can't choose — I love it all!

63

And now...
the silly questions you would be too scared to ask!

1 Do you ever get tired of drawing, because you have to do it all the time?

Well, I take plenty of holidays and when I'm on holiday I'm extremely happy not to do any drawing whatsoever!

2 Who's your favourite cartoon character?

Mr Benn.

3 Would you rather eat ketchup on your cornflakes or 10 bowls of jelly?

I would rather eat the jelly — I love jelly! And when I do eat cornflakes I normally have orange juice on them... really!

SWEET SHOP

4 What's your star sign?

Leo

Drawing by Nick, age 12.

5 Have you ever had 'artist's block' and not known how to draw a character?

I do get artist's block and a walk to the baker's to buy a sticky bun always solves the problem!

6 Have you ever disagreed with Jacqueline about what a character should look like?

I might have suggested once or twice that a character wear slightly different clothes to make for a better illustration. Actually, when I drew the pictures for The Story of Tracy Beaker I put her in a skirt and only later realised that it said jeans in the manuscript. But Jacqueline was very sweet and changed the words so I didn't have to redraw all the artwork.

7 What's the best present you have ever been given?

A rare edition of The General — a picture book that I'd loved as a young child, lost and never seen again.

8 If you were an animal, what would you be?

A well-looked after cat, who spends most of his time asleep in a warm spot.

9 Do you have any unfulfilled ambitions?

To find the perfect flapjack recipe! Mine are never quite right no matter how many times I try.

10 What's your favourite type of holiday?

I'm not at all sporty or outdoorsy but strangely my ideal holiday is to go skiing.

11 If you could only use three colours for illustrating, which colours would you choose?

Black for the lines, then bright orange and light blue for colouring.

12 If you were granted a magic wish, what would you ask for?

I would wish to be able to play the cello superbly. I don't have any musicality at all and I'm completely in awe of people who do.

It's A JW Book Launch!

Sneak a peek behind the scenes!

Jacqueline Wilson

HETTY FEATHER

ILLUSTRATED BY NICK SHARRATT

Will Hetty ever find her true home?

You might think that writing a book is the hard bit, but it doesn't stop there. It's a lot of work to turn a book into a best seller and Jacky's job doesn't stop when she finishes a story.

To sell a book, publishers start with a launch event. For Hetty Feather there was a special *Hetty Feather Day* at the Foundling Museum.

Jacky gave two talks — one in the morning and one in the afternoon — and signed *lots* of books.

There were special Victorian crafts to make, like bonnets decorated with colourful paper flowers, and you could even dress up as a Foundling.

Look at these amazing Hetty Feather biscuits! They were made especially for Jacky, to celebrate her new book.

Naomi

Jacky's lovely publicist, *Naomi*, helps with all the organising. She makes sure Jacky is always in the right place at the right time.

Matron Pigface!

Millie as Hetty

Ten-year-old *Millie Hatland* was chosen to play Hetty for the day.

"I was chosen to play Hetty Feather at the Foundling Museum for Jacky's book launch. I even had to face a real life Matron Stinking Bottomly!

"I was picked out of my drama class because they thought I was like her. I do have red hair like Hetty's!

"I was speechless when I met Jacky — which isn't like me!

"I have 37 Jacqueline Wilson books and now Hetty's my favourite!"

After the launch, Jacky goes on a book tour. She gives talks about her life and writing, and does book signings all over the country.

Wherever she goes, there are hundreds of JW fans there to see her. Here are some at the *Little Darlings* book tour. Everyone is super—excited!

Emily

Lucy

Heather

Maya

Hope

Hannah

Sophie

Su-Ning

Cara

"I enjoy my book events so much because I get to meet all my readers. They're so lovely and often give me gifts — many of them hand—made especially for me.

"Seeing and talking to everyone gives me ideas for new stories and books. Sometimes I even get inspiration from someone's name!"

JW Secret!
Jacky once signed books for **eight** hours!

JW

Lynn

Beth

Ailsa

Book festivals and events take Jacky all over the world. Here she is at a giant sleepover in Australia.

This is an event in Dubai. These girls had dressed up as Jacky's book covers!

Jacky also writes a tour blog for her website. There are stories from every place she visits. Did you attend an event? Check here to see if you've had a mention – www.jacquelinewilson.co.uk/jacqueline–wilson/events/

69

Dani Decides!

Find out **Dani Harmer**'s fave things in our **"this or that"** challenge!

Straight hair or curly?
I've got natural curls and you always want the opposite don't you?!

Dogs or **cats?**
They're less work because you don't have to take them for a walk!

Acting or singing?
That's a really tough one, but probably acting.

iPod or **mobile phone?**

I've got the iPhone which is both, but probably a mobile if I had to choose.

Sweets or crisps? Especially jelly beans!

Parties or **sleepovers?**

I'm a bit old for sleepovers now, so it has to be parties.

Skirts or jeans?

Jeans, I'm a bit of a tomboy.

Dark clothes or sparkly?

Dark clothes - sparkly is a bit too girlie for me.

Strictly Come Dancing or X factor?

But I'd love to have a go at *Strictly* myself.

Sunshine or snow?

It makes everyone happy!

71

I'm Tracy Beaker, the Great Inventor of Extremely Outrageous Dares!

Do You Dare?
Tracy Does!

This is the perfect sleepover party game! Have a laugh and find out funny stories about your friends...

What To Do:

Cut out the 'Dares' and 'Truths' and put them into separate hats. Get all your friends to sit in a circle and choose somebody to start (don't worry, you'll all get a turn). That person has to pick either a **Truth** or a **Dare**. When they've done their task, move clockwise onto the next person. If you run out, just put the paper slips back and start again! **Have fun!**

Dare

1. Get the person on your left to give you a wacky hairstyle like Adele the social worker... and you have to keep it for the whole night! Adele

2. Paint each of your toe or finger nails a different colour!

3. You have to say 'happily ever after' at the end of every sentence until the game is over... LOL!

4. Your friends get to make up a dare for you to do. If you won't do it, pick a Truth.

5. Your friends have to make three different juice mixtures, two of them horrible and one tasty. You have to choose blindfolded which one you will drink... ew!

7. Take a silly picture of you and a friend of your choice and set it as your phone screensaver for the night.

8. Your friends have to pick a song for you to sing. Perform with a hairbrush for 30 seconds!

9. Do an impression of your favourite animal.

10. Go outside the room and dance like you're super-cool for 30 seconds!

Truth

Dare

Dare

Dare

Truth

Dare

Dare

Truth

Truth

1. Would you rather eat a worm sandwich or drink a crushed beetle smoothie?

2. Which Jacqueline Wilson character do you secretly think is most like you?

3. Describe the most horrible smell you have ever come across.

4. Tell your friends one of the scariest stories you have heard.

monster from Mars!

5. Come clean... what's your most embarrassing moment ever?

6. Strictly private! Tell a secret about yourself that nobody else knows.

8. Your friends get to decide on a question to ask you. If you won't answer it, pick a Dare.

9. Go around the room and tell each person your favourite thing about them.

10. Confess... have you ever told a whopping white lie?

Aquarius

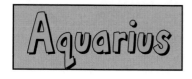

Jan 21 - Feb 19

This year is going to give a big boost to your confidence. Everyone can be shy at times but don't let that hold you back. When you get the opportunity to try something new, don't think twice — just go for it. Remember how Destiny is scared about singing on stage in *Little Darlings*, but when she does it everyone is amazed at her talent? It will be strong self-belief like Destiny's that will help you through.

Best month: June
Lucky colour: red
Important number: 22

Symbols:

Pisces

Feb 20 - Mar 20

You put a lot of time into your friendships, but this year you could try to focus on your family. Families come in all forms, but all are equally important. Whether you have brothers or sisters, or lots of cousins; whether you have a step-parent or live with your grandparents, it's nice to show that you care. Just think how important Cam is to Tracy Beaker! Try to do at least one nice thing for someone in your family each week

Best month: September
Lucky colour: pink
Important number: 3

Symbols:

Aries

Mar 21 - Apr 20

Have you sometimes felt in the shadow of somebody else? Pearl did in *My Sister Jodie*. She wasn't as loud as her sister and shied away from situations where she would be the centre of attention. But just as Pearl learned she had different talents than her sister, this year you will find a new talent that makes you special. It will be something you can do that's different to everyone else. Wonder what it could be...?

Best month: January
Lucky colour: blue
Important number: 15

Symbols:

Taurus

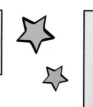

Apr 21 - May 21

This is the year where you will find that one special friend who makes you really happy — or maybe you'll realise you had them all along. Until Cookie found Rhona she thought she would never have a good friend. But by being herself, she found someone who would look out for her, no matter what else happened. Good friends are really important, so make sure you show your friend how much they mean to you.

Best month: October
Lucky colour: silver
Important number: 100

Symbols:

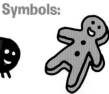

OSCOPES

Find out what exciting things will happen to you this year!

Find your star sign and read your prediction. Then look at your symbols and go to page 77 to find out what they mean.

Gemini

Illustration: Sue Heap.

May 22 - June 21

Which of your friends is so like you that you could be twins? Do people always say you act or sound alike? Well, just like Ruby and Garnet, you may be similar, but you also have big differences. The things that make you unique will become really clear this year. The best thing to do is to be happy going down your new paths, but not to let it come between you. Being different means you have more to share with each other!

Best month: July
Lucky colour: green
Important number: 52

Symbols:

Cancer

June 22 - July 23

Everyone's temper can run away with them sometimes, but you better keep a lid on it! Hetty Feather is really passionate so often says things quickly and gets into trouble for them later. Make sure you think carefully before you speak and it will help prevent problems for you. Sometimes if you feel really angry it helps to write down how you're feeling before you do anything — you'll find you feel calmer already!

Best month: March
Lucky colour: black
Important number: 1

Symbols:

Leo

July 24 - Aug 23

The girls in Sleepovers have The Alphabet Club and love getting their gang together. Have you and your friends ever thought about starting a club? What about a book club? If you have ever read Jacqueline Wilson's magazine you'll know there's loads of stuff to discuss about her books. Being in a club is great fun and a good way of getting everyone involved — this year you could be the one to make it happen!

Best month: May
Lucky colour: purple
Important number: 31

Symbols:

Virgo

Aug 24 - Sept 23

Claire in *The Worry Website* gets really bad nightmares. What scares you? Having fears is fine, but don't let them hold you back. Do you get scared of the dark or of speaking out loud in class? The best way to overcome your fear is to face it head on — try not to ignore things or hide away. When you've done something once it will be so much easier the next time. Maybe you'll wonder what you were ever so scared of!

Best month: December
Lucky colour: white
Important number: 19

Symbols:

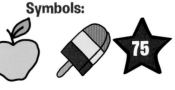

75

Libra

Sept 24 - Oct 23

Have you ever wished you could move away and start over in a new house and at a new school? Lola Rose had to move away really quickly, and even change her name, but that's because things were so bad at home. Do you think you're actually quite lucky with what you have? Sometimes things aren't always better somewhere else. Why not keep a special diary this year where you write down something nice that happens to you each day?

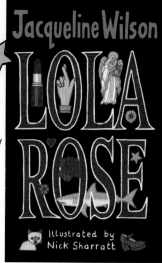

Best month: April
Lucky colour: yellow
Important number: 80

Symbols:

Scorpio

Oct 24 - Nov 22

You like to be different and don't always follow the pack. It's nice to have your own interests, and it can be nice to share them with others too. Maybe you have some interests that you think your friends wouldn't like or would call babyish — the way Sunset feels about her Wardrobe City In *Little Darlings*. But remember how excited Destiny was when she heard about it? Don't be afraid to be show people who you really are.

Best month: August
Lucky colour: orange
Important number: 8

Symbols:

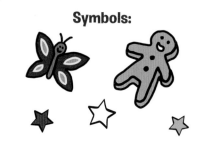

Sagittarius

Nov 23 - Dec 22

Have you ever had to make a really difficult decision? Floss does in *Candyfloss*, where she has to choose to live with her Dad and ends up embarking on an exciting new life. This year is going to be full of important decisions for you, so the best thing to do is to take your time and think about things before you jump in. It's always good to take advice from your friends and family, because they know you so well.

Best month: November
Lucky colour: turquoise
Important number: 50

Symbols:

Capricorn

Dec 23 - Jan 20

Just like Alice and Gemma, you and your friend are well-known besties! It's really important to hold on to good friends like that, but it's also important to be open to new friendships. It won't change the bond the two of you have already. This year someone new will come along, and by the end of the year it'll feel like you've been friends forever. Make sure everyone feels involved and part of the group.

Best month: February
Lucky colour: peach
Important number: 4

Symbols:

JUST ASK!

⭐ Think of the one big question you want to ask about this year.
⭐ Now use your symbols to find your answer.
⭐ Play with your friends by getting them to ask their big questions — you can work out the answer for them!

How to find your answer

Find your symbols, then see which square they meet at in the grid. That's your answer. For example, if you have the burger and ice lolly symbols then your answer would be in this square:

	🍪	🍦	👟
🦋	**Absolutely, positively, definitely YES!**	**Hmmm... maybe, but wish hard!**	**No, this would not be good.**
🐞	**Of course! Did you ever doubt?**	**Absolutely, positively, definitely NO!**	**Probably not, but you never know!**
🍔	**Can't be sure so wait and see.**	**Yes - and that's for sure.**	**No - and you'll be glad of that.**
🍎	**You'll be pleased to hear YES.**	**Uh-oh, that's a NO.**	**It could go either way.**

77

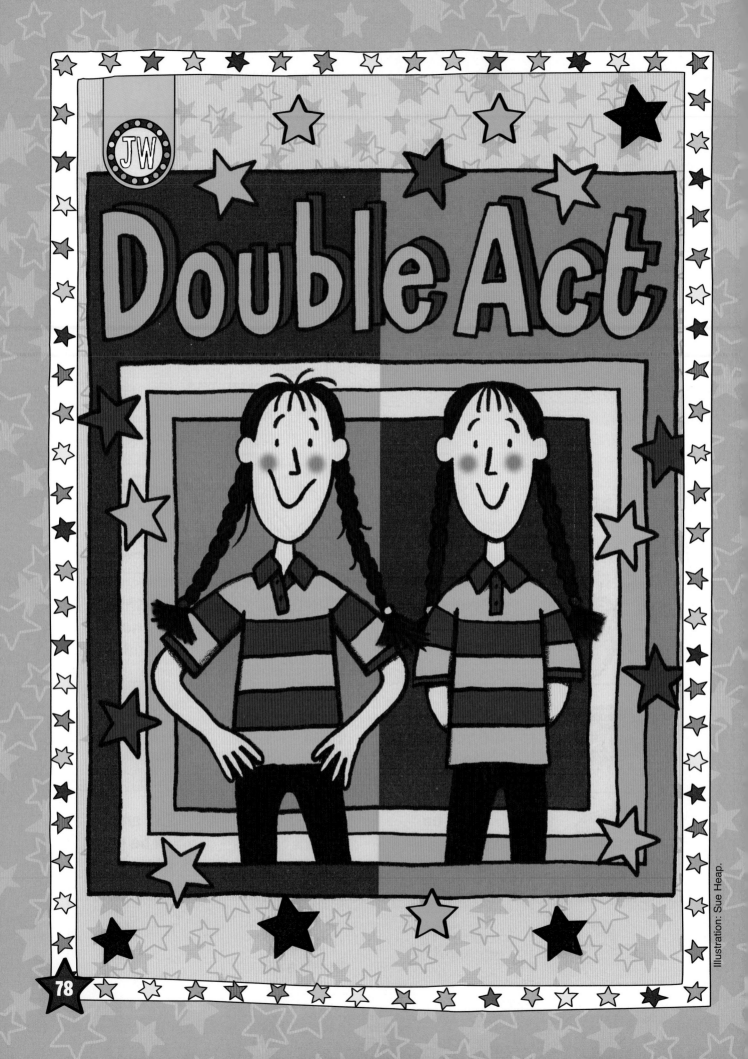

Illustration: Sue Heap.

Fact File

Ruby and Garnet

Hi, I'm Ruby. This is my twin sister, Garnet.

"When we're really pleased about something Garnet puts her fingers at the corners of my mouth and turns it into a huge grin while I do the same to her."

"This is our dad and his girlfriend Rose. She spoils everything..."

"This is our gran. She makes great Sunday dinners!"

WANTED: GIRL TWINS
Sunnylea Productions are going to turn Enid Blyton's much loved *Twins at St Clare's* books into a children's television serial. Auditions start on Monday for the plum parts, the twins themselves, so any likely lively outgoing twin girls aged 10–14 with showbiz ambitions can show up at 10 Newlake Street, London W1, at nine o'clock.

"Garnet and I auditioned to be twins in a TV serial of Enid Blyton's St Clare's."

Illustrations: Sue Heap.

★ How To Draw Ruby And ★ Garnet

Learn how to draw two characters together in just six easy steps.

1 Faintly outline the girls' heads, necks and t-shirts. Add small ears to each head.

2 Draw in the girls' plaited hair and their arms. Leave space at the end of Ruby's arms to draw in her hands.

3 Use short lines to give each girl a fringe and hair at the end of their plaits. Make Ruby's messy and Garnet's neat and tidy! Draw in Ruby's hands so they sit on her hips.

4 Add detail to the girls' hair and their t-shirts. Garnet's is buttoned up neatly whereas Ruby's collar is open.

5 Draw in the girls' facial expressions — give Ruby a longer, more crooked smile.

6 Colour in the twins in matching blue and green striped t-shirts.

Tip: Sketch your drawing in faint pencil first

Now it's
your turn!

Get Crafty!

You can make all this!

PAGE 83

Ribbon Friendship Bracelets

My Special Secrets Box

Strictly Private!

PAGE 84-85

Cute BF Cupcakes

best friends

PAGE 86-87

Butterfly Bookmark

PAGE 88

Ribbon Friendship Bracelets

Make pretty friendship bracelets — one for you, one for your BF!

You'll need:

☑ Elasticated cord ☑ Organza ribbon in two different colours or shades
☑ Coloured beads in different shapes and sizes

1. Cut two lengths of elasticated cord, each around 30cm long. Take one length of cord and tie a knot approx 4cm from the end of it. Make sure your knot is large enough to stop the beads slipping off the end.

2. Choose which colours you'd like to use for your first bracelet. Start threading them on to the elasticated cord and build up a pretty pattern.

3. Tie another knot at the other end of the cord to hold your beads in place.

4. Tie both ends of the cord together to make your bracelet complete.

5. Cut a length of organza ribbon and tie it onto the bracelet in a pretty bow.

Now make another bracelet for your bestie!

83

My Special Secrets

squeak!

Cover a shoebox in bright, colourful wrapping paper or wallpaper. You can use any colours you like!

burger

JW's no.1

yum!

84

Box

Cut out the pictures from the back of this annual and stick them on your box to decorate.

You could also use pictures cut from magazines or even photos.

Strictly Private!

Beaker Is Brilliant!

Totally fantastic

I ♥ reading

glamorous!

icecream

yum!

birthday cake

yum!

Or...

Make A Memory Box!

Fill your box with memories! Keep old birthday cards, special letters and photos of your friends and family in your box. You could also add little souvenirs from a summer holiday or maybe your most favourite drawing.

Add glitz to your box with sparkly stick-on gems.

Cute

best friends

Cupcakes

A sweet way to tell your bestie she's brilliant!

You'll need:

✓ 1 pack of sponge cake mix   ✓ 500g ready-to-roll white icing

✓ Icing sugar   ✓ Food colour   ✓ Cake cases

✓ Decorations - sugar balls, sprinkles, icing pens, sweets

What to do:

1 Follow the instructions to make up the cake mix and bake the cupcakes.

2 Knead the ready to roll icing on a surface sprinkled with icing sugar until it's soft.

Colour some of it by kneading in a couple of drops of food colour.

3 Mix up some water icing by adding tiny drops of water to icing sugar to get a paste.

4 Roll out the icing and cut circles to fit the cupcakes. Stick them on to the cakes with dabs of water icing.

5 Now spell out a message for your BF using the decorations. Use tiny amounts of the water icing to keep things in place.

Butterfly Bookmark

Never lose your place again with this pretty bookmark.

These make great gifts!

You'll need:
✓ A coloured envelope ✓ Coloured card
✓ Elasticated cord ✓ Pretty things for decoration

Slips easily onto the corner of the page!

1. Get your coloured envelope and cut the bottom corner off to make a triangle. This will be the base of your bookmark.

2. Fold your coloured card in half and draw one side of a butterfly. Cut it out and unfold to get your butterfly. Then cut a smaller butterfly from a different coloured piece of card.

3. Place the smaller butterfly shape on top of the bigger one. Tie your cord around the middle of the two butterfly shapes to hold them in position. Leave the ends of the cord longer to give your butterfly antennae!

4. Decorate your butterfly with gems, stickers, pens or glitter glue.

5. Finally, stick your butterfly firmly to the envelope corner and ta-da! You have a gorgeous butterfly bookmark!

Cut and stick pictures just for you!

birthday cake — yum!

Beaker Is Brilliant!

squeak!

Triple Gold Star

burger — yum!

Super-cool

icecream — yum!

Strictly Private!

jelly spider — yum!

JW's no.1 fan!

89

I ♥ JW

S-o-o-o glamorous!

I ♥ Tracy Beaker

chocolate bar

yum!

Totally fantastic

spaceship

cool!

I ♥ reading

91

POSTAGE IS FREE!

NEVER MISS AN ISSUE - SIGN UP NOW TO The Official Jacqueline Wilson Mag

SAVE £12
ON A 1 YEAR SUBSCRIPTION!*
* UK prices

1 year costs £40 - £10 per quarter by direct debit

Full of brilliant features!

- ✓ Exclusive writing tips from Jacqueline Wilson
- ✓ Draw with Nick Sharratt
- ✓ Fun flowcharts and puzzles
- ✓ Learn all about Jacky's brilliant books

HOW TO SIGN UP

Ask an adult to –

- Log on to www.jw-mag.com/subs
- Call free on our credit/debit card hotline 0800 318 846 (Freephone from UK landlines only)
- Pay by direct debit (1 year min). Call for a mandate.
- Please quote JWAN when ordering